by
Sean Taylor

pictures by
Edel Rodriguez

ROBOMOP

Dial Books for Young Readers an imprint of Penguin Group (USA) Inc.

DIAL BOOKS FOR YOUNG READERS
A division of Penguin Young Readers Group • Published by The Penguin Group • Penguin Group (USA) Inc., 375 Hudson Street, New York, NY 10014, U.S.A. • Penguin Group (Canada), 90 Eglinton Avenue East, Suite 700, Toronto, Ontario, Canada M4P 2Y3 (a division of Pearson Penguin Canada Inc.) • Penguin Books Ltd, 80 Strand, London WC2R 0RL, England • Penguin Ireland, 25 St. Stephen's Green, Dublin 2, Ireland (a division of Penguin Books Ltd) • Penguin Group (Australia), 250 Camberwell Road, Camberwell, Victoria 3124, Australia (a division of Pearson Australia Group Pty Ltd) • Penguin Books India Pvt Ltd, 11 Community Centre, Panchsheel Park, New Delhi - 110 017, India • Penguin Group (NZ), 67 Apollo Drive, Rosedale, Auckland 0632, New Zealand (a division of Pearson New Zealand Ltd) • Penguin Books (South Africa) (Pty) Ltd, 24 Sturdee Avenue, Rosebank, Johannesburg 2196, South Africa • Penguin Books Ltd, Registered Offices: 80 Strand, London WC2R 0RL, England

Designed by Lily Malcom • Text set in Archer • Manufactured in China on acid-free paper

10 9 8 7 6 5 4 3 2 1

Library of Congress Cataloging-in-Publication Data
Taylor, Sean, date.
Robomop / by Sean Taylor ; pictures by Edel Rodriguez.
p. cm.
Summary: A robotic mop, assigned to clean a basement restroom, yearns to feel the sunshine, see the world, and more, but when he thinks he has finally escaped, his life is not as he expected, until a friend helps him out.
ISBN 978-0-8037-3411-1 (hardcover)
[1. Robots—Fiction. 2. Mops and mopsticks—Fiction. 3. Humorous stories.] I. Rodriguez, Edel, ill.
II. Title.
PZ7.T21783Rob 2013 [E]—dc23 2012012901

The illustrations in this book were created with oil-based woodblock ink printed on paper, combined with digital media.

PEARSON
ALWAYS LEARNING

For Milla
—ST

For Gabrielle
and Sofia
—ER

There I was, a very hardworking Robomop.
Slightly dented from the odd small accident,
but good at my job, which is cleaning.

And do you know what I had to clean?

A bathroom.

In a basement.

It wasn't funny one slightest bit in the least!
No fresh air. No friends.
All day every day,

washing,

sloshing,

rubbing,

scrubbing,
slopping,
and
mopping.

How would *you* feel about that?
Well, I'll tell you how *I* felt.

I FELT LIKE ESCAPING!

But Robomops cannot get up steps.

The Inspector of Public Restrooms came every Friday to see how clean I was keeping things.

So I tried a clever tactic.

I ran over a bag of potato chips until it jammed in my lateral vacuum vent.

As planned, it made a sound like I was broken.

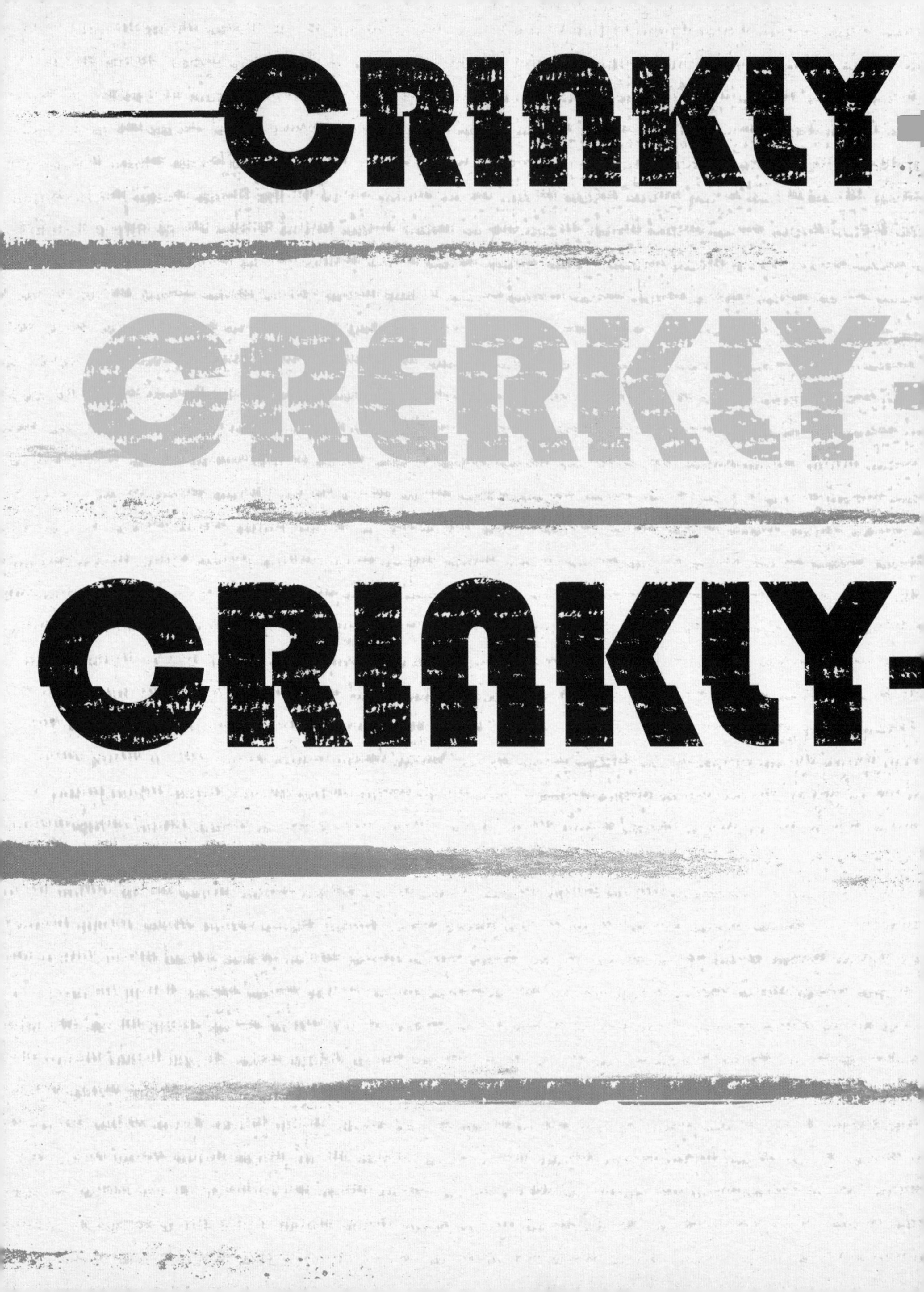
CRINKLY-
CREAKLY-
CRINKLY-

CRACKLY-

CRACKLY-

CRACKLY-

CRERK!
INSPECTOR

I hoped that the inspector would take me out to be fixed—and then I could make my escape!

Instead, he put a cardboard box over me to keep the noise down while he inspected.

But I was not to be defeated.
Not in the least bit.

You see, a man came in
with a very big duffel bag,
and I tried to escape by
hiding inside it.

Unfortunately, he noticed.

Then, once each month, the window cleaner cheerfully came to squeegee-and-so-forth the windows.

He always brought his radio, which played a sort of honky-tonk music.

If I sometimes did a small honky-tonk dance to the tunes, you should have heard how loudly he laughed. And once he said,

"You'd better stop doing
that, my friend, or
someone'll probably *sell
you to the circus!*"

So I did *not* stop doing it.

In fact, I did a small honky-tonk dance every time somebody arrived—

and I hoped they *would* sell me to the circus.

But they didn't.

Oh dear. I was completely gloomy,
and in a sad pickle.

How was I ever going see the world, feel
the sunshine, and fall in love?

I was stuck down there,
well and truly, with an awful case of
Robomop-basement-bathroom blues.

Then, one day, everything changed.

To my greatest amazement, the Inspector of Public Restrooms arrived, and under his arm was a completely brand-new BIO-MORPHIC BELLEBOT CLEANERETTE.

I couldn't believe my lucky day! A friend! For me! I was overcome with excitement, so much that I had an odd small accident.

But the problem that followed was a worse problem. The inspector put down the BIO-MORPHIC BELLEBOT CLEANERETTE and, as soon as he could, he picked me up!

He put me under his arm!

He carried me up the steps!

And he threw me away with the garbage, which I was not ready for. It was not right in the least bit.

"I am a very hardworking Robomop, and I am not broken at all! It is not fair to throw me away!"

I was up there in the sunshine, seeing the whole wide world at last. But it wasn't like the dream-come-true that I had been dreaming.

I tried to get down. But Robomops cannot get out of garbage cans.

There was nothing left on earth that I could do.

And what's more, the window cleaner cheerfully arrived. He had come to squeegee-and-so-forth the windows, but the Inspector of Public Restrooms said to him,

"I am sorry. We don't require your services. The new cleaning robot can reach the windows."

That was that. I looked at the window cleaner. He looked at me. We were stuck there, well and truly, with an awful case of *window-cleaner-and-Robomop-lost-job blues*.

So it was a surprise when he cheerfully picked me up and carried me off down the street.

I thought he would probably sell me to the circus.

But no.

He took me to his home.

And I think it is quite a good one. The window cleaner has a family with one mother, two girls, two boys, and one dog.

All of them seem to like honky-tonk music. So the radio is often playing. Which makes my job very much easier, I think.

A fast wash, slosh, rub, scrub, slop, mop, and everything is clean.

What's more, if I sometimes do a small honky-tonk dance to the tunes, you should hear how loudly everyone laughs.

And you know what?

I think I am falling in love with the vacuum cleaner.